The GLAM World Tour

by Rachel Werner
illustrated by Octavia Ink

CAPSTONE EDITIONS
a capstone imprint

On the glam world tour, people gather

. . . who **primp,**
preen,
shine,

with native sheen. **Mini queens . . .**

Our tents displaying charms from home.

Rows upon rows

Filled with floral scents,

or new trends shared **across the seas.**

From Tehran

to Lagos

to London

to NYC.

Bountiful 'fros **bop** down jazzy streets.

AFRO ('fro) a full crown of naturally, tightly curled hair styled into a round shape

Dazzling corkscrews twirl, then . . .

S-P-R-I-N-G!

CORKSCREWS tight curls or small braids that hold a springy shape and radiate around the scalp

Others dig the luster of whimsical weaves.

WEAVES human or artificial hairpieces used to change the length, fullness, or overall look of one's natural hair

Or fresh, tight locs that **S-W-I-N-G** as we walk.

LOCS (also called dreadlocks) a hairstyle created by twisting or braiding sections of hair until bound together like rope

Mehndi flashing as fingers snap,

MEHNDI a style of decorative body art often used for celebratory occasions in India, Pakistan, and Nepal

HENNA a reddish-brown dye made from a tropical plant used on hair and to make temporary tattoos for special occasions (like weddings) in certain parts of the Middle East, Africa, and India

Henna **gleaming** as hands clap.

Honey,
    caramel,
        almond,
            and chocolate skin.

Shimmer from the **natural radiance** we were born in.

Harmonizing with bold lips in cherry and orange hues, making kohl-lined eyes beam above bronzed cheeks.

We **sparkle** by embracing our true identities, celebrating each body's unique abilities.

And by welcoming new friends from wherever they come.

Because inner **beauty** comes from accepting—

To both of my mothers, Veronica and Lucinda: THANKS for teaching me how to be BEAUTIFUL—inside and out. —RW

RACHEL WERNER has written numerous picture books, including *Floods* and *Moving & Grooving to Fillmore's Beat*, as well as the nonfiction middle grade title *Glow & Grow: A Brown Girl's Positive Body Guide* and the forthcoming nonfiction YA title *Beauty Emancipation*. She is on faculty for Hugo House in Seattle, Lighthouse Writers Workshop in Denver, and the Loft Literary Center in Minneapolis, where she leads curricula to educate writers and content producers in marketing their work.

To my grandma, who taught me how to shine. —OI

OCTAVIA INK is a Michigan-based fine artist, illustrator, and printmaker. A lover of every yellow hue, her illustrations are vibrant and filled with color. Her work is rooted in visual storytelling. She uses her illustrations to tell dynamic stories that reflect her community, celebrating color in more ways than one. Armed with a pencil, she wants to draw a better future filled with joy, positivity, liberation, and even brighter colors.

Published by Capstone Editions, an imprint of Capstone
1710 Roe Crest Drive, North Mankato, Minnesota 56003
capstonepub.com

Text copyright © 2025 Rachel Werner
Illustrations copyright © 2025 Octavia Ink

All rights reserved. No part of this publication may be reproduced in whole or in part, or stored in a retrieval system, or transmitted in any form or by any means, electronic, mechanical, photocopying, recording, or otherwise, without written permission of the publisher.

Library of Congress Cataloging-in-Publication Data
is available on the Library of Congress website.
ISBN: 9781630792947 (hardcover)
ISBN: 9781630792961 (ebook PDF)

Summary: Written in the spirit of spoken word, the stunning variation of beauty norms around the world are showcased and celebrated as inclusive, not divisive, in this compelling picture book.

Designed by Nathan Gassman